LATKI and THE LIGHTNING LIZARD

LATKI AND THE LIGHTNING LIZARD

By Betty Baker

Illustrated by Donald Carrick

Latki's father is a woodcutter. One day, in a remote part of the mountain, he begins to chop a large tree stump. With a crackling and a blinding flash of light, a giant lizard appears and stands tall above the frightened man. "You are destroying my home. You have shaken and broken things inside. You must pay for the damage," says the angry lizard. "Bring me one of your daughters!"

The woodcutter dares not disobey. Daughter after daughter is taken up the mountain. The first is too noisy; the second is too fat; the third—gentle Seri—is accepted and must stay in the enchanted canyon as the lizard's housekeeper. But Latki, the youngest, misses her favorite sister. Armed only with a spear made of yucca stem and the ability to speak with animals, she sets out on a strange and dangerous journey to rescue Seri from the lightning lizard.

BETTY BAKER

Latki and the Lightning Lizard

ILLUSTRATED BY DONALD CARRICK

Macmillan Publishing Co., Inc., New York

Collier Macmillan Publishers, London

Macmillan Publishing Co., Inc.
866 Third Avenue, New York, N.Y. 10022
Collier Macmillan Canada, Ltd.

Printed in the United States of America

10 9 8 7 6 5 4 3 2 1

LIBRARY OF CONGRESS CATALOGING IN PUBLICATION DATA
Baker, Betty.
    Latki and the lightning lizard.
    SUMMARY: A resourceful young girl rescues her older
sister from the magical Lightning Lizard with the aid of
an eagle, a lion, and an ant.
    [1. Fantasy] I. Carrick, Donald. II. Title.
PZ7.B1693Lat   [E]   79-11197   ISBN 0-02-708210-5

For Lecia

—D.C.

In a mud brick house in a red rock canyon in the side of Mingus Mountain lived Latki, her father and her three older sisters. Latki loved the canyon. Her sisters did not.

Her eldest sister was very pretty, with large dark eyes and long black hair. But she was not happy. Once Latki found her beside the spring, combing her hair and crying.

"What is the matter?" said Latki.

Her sister said, "I want to live in town."

"Why?" said Latki. "Our canyon has rocks that change color with the light and season. It has moving shadows and helpful creatures, a good spring and our garden. Does the town have these?"

"No," said her sister, "but it has tortoise shell combs to hold up my hair and earrings with jewels that glow."

"The canyon has those, too," said Latki.

Her sister laughed.

Latki could not find tortoises small enough, but
she coaxed two pretty brown lizards to sit on her
head, their claws tucked under to hold up her hair.
She asked two butterflies with bright glowing wings
to perch on her ears. Then she went back to her sister.

"Look," she said. "You do not need to move to town."

Her sister screamed and threw her comb at the lizards.

"Take those ugly creatures away!" she cried.

Latki had to apologize three times, once to the lizards who were used to being chased and twice to the butterflies who were not.

Her second sister was fat and did the cooking. But she was always searching for something to eat. One winter Latki found her sitting on a sunny rock chewing willow twigs.

"You cannot be hungry," Latki told her. "Why are you eating that?"

"There is nothing else to do here," said her sister. "If I lived in town, I could visit for coffee or afternoon tea. There'd be dinners and dances with interesting people. I'd always have someone to talk with."

"The canyon is filled with interesting creatures," said Latki. "You can talk with them."

"Nobody talks to animals," said her sister.

"I do," said Latki.

Her sister laughed so hard she slid off the rock and Latki had to call her other sisters to help get her up.

But the next sister, Seri, never screamed or laughed at Latki. She listened gravely when Latki told her what animals said and did. She helped Latki make stick dolls, leaf bread and mud soup. They played games along the canyon walls and strung necklaces of seeds and crimson berries.

Then Seri began telling stories, tales of far lands and distant times. Sometimes Latki found her sitting at the end of the canyon, staring down at the town.

Once Latki said, "I suppose you want to live there, too."

"I do not know," Seri told her. "I have never been there."

"Let's play hide-the-beetle," said Latki.

"Not now," said her sister and she breathed a deep and lingering sigh.

Latki asked an old chulo about it but the ring-tailed animal told her not to worry.

"It is something that comes to us all in the spring," she said. "It will pass. Just wait."

Latki did. But while she waited, Seri went away.

Latki's father was a woodcutter. He left the canyon before dawn and often did not return until Latki was asleep. One day, in his search for firewood, he climbed to a strange part of the mountain and found a large tree stump. The woodcutter unslung his ax and began to chop. There was a crackling and a blinding flash of light.

When his eyes cleared, the woodcutter saw a huge lizard standing on two legs like a man. He wore a long chain tunic, the links set with precious stones. Jeweled rings were on his claws, and the hilt of his sword had an emerald large as a plum.

"You are destroying my home," said the lizard.
"You have shaken and broken things inside, and here
you have split the wall. You must pay for the damage."

"I have no money," said the woodcutter.

"Then I will take your donkey," said the lizard.

"Not my donkey!" said the woodcutter. "Without it, I cannot carry enough wood to the town. I have four daughters. They will starve!"

"Then bring me one of your daughters," said the lizard. "I need someone to clean my house and prepare my meals."

The woodcutter begged and pleaded but the lizard said, "Tomorrow," and with a crackle and flash of light was gone. The woodcutter dared not disobey. Such a creature could find and destroy them all. Early the next morning, while Latki slept, he took his eldest daughter up the mountain. When she saw the lizard, she began to scream.

"She is too noisy," said the lizard. "Bring me a quiet one."

And he left in a crackling flash of light.

Next dawn, before Latki woke, the woodcutter took his second eldest. She did not scream when she saw the lizard but she could not squeeze down the hollow stump into the lizard's house.

"Bring me a thin one," said the lizard, and vanished in a crackling light.

The next morning, when Latki woke, Seri was gone. The following morning, she had not returned.

"She has gone to be a housekeeper," her sisters said, but they would not tell her where. Latki stayed up late to ask her father but all he said was, "You must tend the garden now."

The next night, Latki waited until everyone was asleep. Then she crept outside to talk with the donkey.

"Where did you leave my sister?" she said.

"With a giant lizard," the donkey told her. "One that cracks and flashes lightning."

"Where does this lightning lizard live?" said Latki.

"Up the mountain behind an arch."

"How do you get there?" said Latki.

"Up a long and winding ledge."

"Where is the ledge?"

"Up the mountain."

Latki could learn no more. None of the canyon's creatures could tell her where Seri was. So early one morning, Latki sneaked all the corn cakes off the table, took up her spear made of yucca stem and started up the mountain.

She watched for jays and ravens, but when she asked about the lightning lizard, they flew away without answering. When she stopped at midday to eat, she found only ground squirrels, a tarantula and a gopher snake, small creatures who seldom wandered far from their burrows. But the snake had been frightened when Seri, her father and the donkey passed. He pointed himself in the proper direction and Latki soon came to the ledge.

Up and around she went, a red rock wall on one side and a long steep drop on the other, using her spear as a walking stick. Beyond one of the turns, Latki heard shrieks and yowling. She turned her spear, ready to throw, and advanced around the curve.

An eagle and a mountain lion were fighting over
a dead animal. They tugged and pulled at opposite
sides, flapping and hissing, clawing and shouting
insults. Latki dared not try to pass.

"Stop!" she told them. She swished her spear at the
eagle and poked the lion with its point. "Stop it, I say!"

"Who are you?" said the mountain lion.

"I am Latki. The lightning lizard has forced my
sister to keep his house. I am going to rescue her."

Bird and animal stared at her. Still staring, the
eagle folded its wings and sank to the carcass. The
lion turned and swiped a paw at the bird.

"That's mine," he snarled.

"Mine!" shrieked the eagle.

"Stop it!" Latki thumped her spear on the ground.

"Go find the lizard," said the lion.

"I can't while you're fighting," said Latki. "Why don't you share the food? I'll divide it for you."

She pushed the pieces of meat with her spear. "This pile is yours," she told the eagle.

"You're very generous with my food," said the mountain lion.

"There's more than you can eat," said Latki.

"Not if everyone keeps stealing it." He aimed a paw at a bit of meat being carried away by an ant. Latki tried to stop the blow. The paw broke the spear but the ant crawled out from under the shattered end. Latki finished sorting the meat.

"You get the large pile," she told the lion. "The eagle gets the smaller. The ant will clean up the scraps. While you eat, I will tell you about my sister."

The ant climbed up the spear to listen. When Latki finished, the lion said, "I will tell you this. The lightning lizard can only be slain when hit on the head with a gorgosaur egg."

Then he jumped over Latki and followed the ledge down around the curve.

"Thank you for your help," Latki called after him.

"That wasn't any help," said the eagle. "There are no more gorgosaurs."

"But there is an egg," said the ant. "The lightning lizard has it. He keeps it in his parlor in a silver box."

She pulled an antenna from her head and held it out to Latki. "When you put this under your tongue," she said, "you will become an ant."

"Thank you, ant, for your help," said Latki and she rolled the antenna in a penstemon blossom and stored it in her pocket.

"What help is that?" said the eagle. She dug through her breast feathers with her beak and pulled out one tiny feather. "When this is under your tongue," she said, "you will become an eagle. That is help worth having."

"Thank you, kind eagle," said Latki.

She placed the feather beside the blossom, shouldered her broken spear and went on, up and around the narrowing ledge.

It wasn't far to a cleft in the wall topped by a long flat stone. The stone could not have fallen by accident.

Latki crept through the arch, careful as a coyote. She found herself in a bowl-shaped canyon more brilliantly colored than her own. Purple, red and orange boulders were tumbled at odd angles and weathered into huge stone animals. They seemed to be the only creatures in the canyon. Latki heard no others, not a buzz or chirp or whistle. Yet the grass grew thick and high as her knees.

She moved from stone to stone. Then she saw her sister climb out of a stump dragging a long, heavy rug. She spread the rug on the grass and beat dust from it with a stick.

"Seri!" Latki ran to her sister, waving her spear.

Seri dropped the beating stick. "Latki," she cried, "why are you here?"

"I am rescuing you," she said. "Where is the lizard's parlor?"

"I don't know," said her sister. "There are so many rooms with so many things and I've just begun to clean them." She breathed a deep and weary sigh.

"We must find a silver box," said Latki and she told her what the lion and ant had said.

"We must hurry," said Seri. "The lizard returns each day at sunset."

Latki followed her sister down into the tree stump and past room after room filled with things. One room had only shells, some as fine as the ant's antenna and one large enough to hold Latki. Another room was filled with rocks, clear and sparkling, colored and shining. There was a room full of lutes and other instruments and one with nothing but feathers.

The next had furniture made of animal horns. On a table was a carved silver box. It was locked.

Seri began to cry.

"I can open it," said Latki.

She pried a splinter from the broken end of her spear and laid it on the table. Then she took the blossom out of her pocket and carefully unfolded the petals.

"Be careful where you step," she told her sister. "I am going to become an ant."

She put the antenna under her tongue. The room seemed to burst around her. Everything looked strange and she could not find the legs of the table. A pink mountain came down in front of her.

"Climb on my finger," said Seri, and she lifted Latki to the table.

Latki carried the splinter into the lock. She pushed and levered and pried until the lock clicked. Seri opened the silver box and Latki ran up to look. On a nest of green velvet lay a large egg, its shell marbled with brown. It was warm under Latki's ant feet.

She returned to the floor, took the antenna from under her tongue and became herself. Then she rewrapped the antenna and placed it back in her pocket.

"The egg is too large," said Seri. "The lizard will see it in my hand and be gone before I can strike."

"Then I will sneak up and hit him while you talk," said Latki.

"He is taller than you," said her sister.

"Then I must hide and hit him," said Latki. "But where?"

"He always appears in the kitchen," said Seri. "He orders his dinner and then inspects my cleaning."

The kitchen had a great tall cupboard topped with high carved molding. Latki changed to an ant, ran up the cupboard and took the antenna from her mouth.

Seri climbed on a stool and handed Latki the egg. "We must be quiet now. The sun is setting and the lizard arrives without warning."

Latki placed the antenna in easy reach. Gently she held the egg and settled herself. Seri stood beside the cupboard, arranging dishes inside. There was a crackling and a flash of light and the lizard appeared beside Seri.

"I am hungry. Prepare grubs and grain on gripple sprouts. Where did you clean today?" he said.

While Seri told the lizard, Latki reached down and smashed the egg on his head. The lizard roared. He crackled and sizzled and sprayed green sparks.

There was yellow smoke and a terrible smell. When it cleared, nothing remained of the lightning lizard but his sword and rings and tunic on a pile of glistening cinders.

Latki grinned. "Now you can come home," she said.

Then the cupboard began to shake. The walls shuddered. Latki popped the antenna into her mouth and ran down to the floor. Just as she became herself again, the cupboard crashed beside her. Chunks of dirt fell from the ceiling.

"Get out!" said Seri and gave Latki a push toward the stairs.

Latki dropped the ant's antenna but dared not stop to search for it. She climbed out of the shaking stump, her sister not far behind her.

The ground heaved beneath their feet and the stone animals began to walk. With great jerking movements, a bear came toward them. Seri screamed.

"Run!" said Latki. "I will protect you."

She placed the eagle feather under her tongue. She felt light and eager to fly, but it took longer than she'd thought to get into the air. She swooped at the bear's head just as it reached for Seri. It turned away from Latki's eagle claws and attacked a giant armadillo.

Latki flew around her sister until Seri reached
the arch and climbed over the fallen stone. Then she
soared over the canyon and watched the walls crumble
and slide, crushing the beasts of stone and covering
the lizard's house forever.

Latki changed back to herself and walked with her sister through the night. Seri sang. Latki talked to creatures she'd never met before. They reached home in time for breakfast. Their father and sisters stared when they walked in the door.

"I have rescued Seri," said Latki, "and slain the lightning lizard."

Seri had snatched up the lizard's sword, his rings and jeweled tunic. The woodcutter retired and they moved into town with houses all around them. The eldest sister wed the mayor's son and the next eldest married the baker. They went to coffees and lunches and teas and dinners and crowded parties. Often Seri went with them.

Only Latki missed the canyon, its creatures and spring and colored rocks. But she still had the eagle feather. When Seri dressed and drove off in the carriage, Latki put the feather under her tongue and flew back to the canyon and nobody knew she was gone.